Governing the United States

Ask the Mayor

Christy Mihaly

ROurke
Educational Media
rourkeeducationalmedia.com

A Division of
Carson
Dellosa
Education

BEFORE AND DURING READING ACTIVITIES

Before Reading: *Building Background Knowledge and Vocabulary*

Building background knowledge can help children process new information and build upon what they already know. Before reading a book, it is important to tap into what children already know about the topic. This will help them develop their vocabulary and increase their reading comprehension.

Questions and Activities to Build Background Knowledge:

1. Look at the front cover of the book and read the title. What do you think this book will be about?
2. What do you already know about this topic?
3. Take a book walk and skim the pages. Look at the table of contents, photographs, captions, and bold words. Did these text features give you any information or predictions about what you will read in this book?

Vocabulary: *Vocabulary Is Key to Reading Comprehension*

Use the following directions to prompt a conversation about each word.

- Read the vocabulary words.
- What comes to mind when you see each word?
- What do you think each word means?

Vocabulary Words:
- city council
- councilmember
- executive
- legislative
- limit
- local
- residents
- veto

During Reading: *Reading for Meaning and Understanding*

To achieve deep comprehension of a book, children are encouraged to use close reading strategies. During reading, it is important to have children stop and make connections. These connections result in deeper analysis and understanding of a book.

Close Reading a Text

During reading, have children stop and talk about the following:

- Any confusing parts
- Any unknown words
- Text to text, text to self, text to world connections
- The main idea in each chapter or heading

Encourage children to use context clues to determine the meaning of any unknown words. These strategies will help children learn to analyze the text more thoroughly as they read.

When you are finished reading this book, turn to the next-to-last page for **Text-Dependent Questions** and an **Extension Activity**.

TABLE OF CONTENTS

What the Mayor Does

The mayor is an elected head of a city. They are "the face of the city." What does this mean? Ask the mayor!

What is the mayor's job?

The mayor leads the **executive** branch of city government. Mayors help run cities. They work to help their cities' **residents**. They keep an eye on how much money their cities spend. They help get new laws passed.

They Love a Parade!
Millions of people live in big cities. Some small towns have just a few residents. Big-city mayors are well paid. Some small-town mayors are not paid at all. But all mayors can march in hometown parades.

The mayor represents the city. They are part of the **local** government. They meet and speak with people from other cities to talk about problems and projects.

What are the requirements to be mayor?

Most cities say a mayor must be at least 18 or 21 years old. A mayor must be able to vote in their city. And they should want to help the people of the city. Here are some past and present mayors from across the country.

Washington, D.C., mayor Muriel Bowser helps distribute food.

Lori Lightfoot
56th Mayor of Chicago, IL

London Breed
45th Mayor of
San Francisco, CA

John Tyler Hammons
47th Mayor of Muskogee, OK
elected at age 19

Aja Brown
18th Mayor of Compton, CA

First U.S. Woman Mayor
In 1887, Susanna Madora Salter became
mayor of Argonia, Kansas. She was
America's first woman mayor.

Who does the mayor work with?

The mayor works with the **city council**. That is how they help to get new laws passed. Members of the city council vote on laws.

The council is the **legislative** branch of city government. It decides how the city spends money. It makes decisions about how the city will use its land and repair its roads and bridges. It helps with projects that are important to city residents.

   Many mayors also have employees and volunteers who work for them. Mayors work with and for the people who live in their cities.

What does the mayor do at work?

The mayor studies the city's problems. They run city council meetings. They meet with people who want to build things in town. They meet with city workers.

The mayor sometimes posts on social media. They talk to reporters for news stories. The mayor stays busy!

Q&A with Mayor Rochelle Nason, Albany, California

Q: *What's your favorite part about being mayor?*
A: *Talking with people in my town. We talk about how to make Albany a better place. We care about our town and about each other.*

The Mayor's Powers

Do all mayors have the same power?

No. Big-city mayors often have greater powers than mayors of small cities. They can hire and fire city workers. They can **veto** laws passed by the city council.

Los Angeles Mayor
From 1973 to 1993, Tom Bradley was mayor of Los Angeles, California. He was the first African-American mayor of L.A. He was also the first L.A. mayor elected to five terms.

In many cities, the city council has more power than the mayor. Voters elect the city council. Then, the council picks one **councilmember** to be mayor.

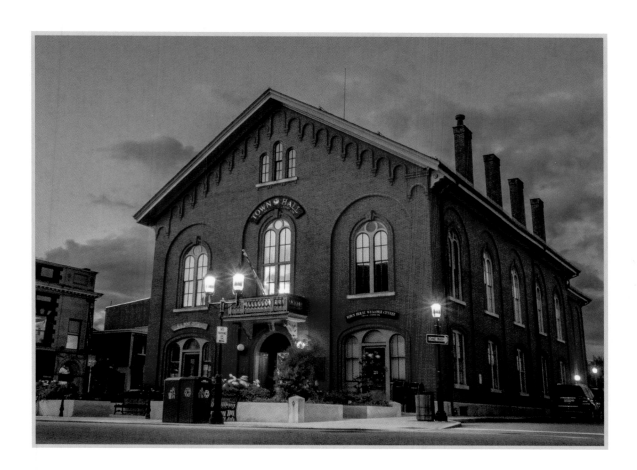

Who tells the mayor what to do?

The city council can sometimes tell the mayor "no." It can vote against laws the mayor wants.

City voters have a say too. It is important for the mayor to work with the city's residents. They are the voters who decide if the mayor will keep their job.

Some state laws **limit** what mayors can do. Here's an example. Many states require a person to be 16 years old to drive a car. If a mayor wanted to let eight-year-olds drive in their city, that would not be allowed.

Does the mayor have other roles?

Yes! The mayor attends special events. They join city celebrations. They cut red ribbons to open new buildings. When important people visit the city, the mayor greets them.

Sister Cities

Many cities have "sister cities" around the world. Groups of people from sister cities visit one another. They share music, art, and ideas. Often, the mayor leads sister city trips to other countries.

Mayors also step up in difficult times. If a hurricane hits town, the mayor visits damaged homes. They work hard to get help for the people.

Interesting Things About Being Mayor

Where does the mayor live?

A few mayors live in special houses owned by their cities. The mayor of Detroit, Michigan, is one of these. The mayor and their family live in a large house called Manoogian Mansion. It has plenty of space for meetings and other events.

Manoogian Mansion

Most mayors stay in their regular homes. When he was mayor of Newark, New Jersey, Cory Booker did not live in a mansion. He stayed in his apartment.

Cory Booker

What city do you live in? Who is your mayor?

Do you think something is great about your town? Do you see a problem that could be fixed? Tell your mayor!

Government of the United States

Mayors work in the executive branch of government. Can you find the mayor in the chart?

	Legislative Branch Makes the laws.	Executive Branch Carries out the laws.	Judicial Branch Decides what laws mean.
Federal Governs the whole country.	**Congress** Includes Senators and members of the House of Representatives.	**The President** Works with cabinet members such as the U.S. Attorney General.	**U.S. Courts** Judges work at many courts, including the U.S. Supreme Court.
State Governs each of the 50 states.	**State Legislature** Representatives work at the capitol building in each state's capital city.	**The Governor** Works with many officials such as the Secretary of State and the State Attorney General.	**State Courts** Include the highest court in the state—the state Supreme Court.
Local Governs each village, town, or city.	**City Council** Representatives make rules about how land is used, where roads will be built, and more.	**The City Mayor** Is in charge of the police department, the parks department, and more.	**Local Courts** Judges rule on cases that involve city laws and crimes that are less serious.

Glossary

city council (SIT-ee KOUN-suhl): a group of people elected to help run a city by passing city laws and performing other duties

councilmember (KOUN-suhl-mem-bur): a person who is part of a council; they help make decisions for the city

executive (ig-ZEK-yuh-tiv): relating to the branch of government that carries out the laws

legislative (LEJ-is-lay-tiv): relating to the branch of government that makes new laws

limit (LIM-uht): to hold back or reduce

local (LOH-kuhl): relating to an area nearby, or at the city level

residents (REZ-i-duhnts): people who live in a certain place

veto (VEE-toh): to stop a law that has been passed, so it does not go into effect

Index

Text-Dependent Questions

1. What can mayors do to help their cities?

2. What are some limits on a mayor's power?

3. Name some people who work with the mayor.

4. Would you like to be a mayor? Why or why not?

5. Would you rather be the mayor of a big city or a small city? Why?

Extension Activity

Do you know the name of the mayor of your city or town? If not, look it up on the city or town website, in a directory, or ask a librarian, teacher, or other adult. Write a letter to the mayor about a local problem you see or an idea you have to improve life in your town.

ABOUT THE AUTHOR

Christy Mihaly has never been a mayor, but she has helped mayors solve some challenging problems. For many years, she was a lawyer for cities and towns. Christy has degrees in policy studies and law. She is the author of many books for young readers that are about our society and politics. She wrote *Free for You and Me*, a picture book about the First Amendment. Find out more or say hello at her website: www.christymihaly.com.

www.rourkeeducationalmedia.com

PHOTO CREDITS: cover: ©Benedetta Barbanti; page 4: ©AfricaImages; page 5: ©Roberto Galan; page 6: ©Phil Pasquini; page 7: ©wiki; page 8: ©stock_photo_world; page 9: ©avid_creative; page 10: ©Rawpixel.com; page 11: ©Brandon Laufenberg; page 12 (Bradley): ©Bart Sherkow; page 12: ©TheCrimsonRibbon; page 13: ©HABESEN; page 14: ©JasonDoiy; page 15: ©Kate_Sept2004; page 16: ©David Parsons; page 17a: ©Anna Bryukhanova; page 17b: ©Chuyn; page 18: ©wiki; page 19: ©Ryan deBeradinis; page 20: ©Steve Debenport

Edited by: Madison Capitano
Cover and interior design by: Rhea Magaro-Wallace

Library of Congress PCN Data

Ask the Mayor / Christy Mihaly (Governing the United States)
ISBN 978-1-73162-902-9 (hard cover)
ISBN 978-1-73162-856-5 (soft cover)
ISBN 978-1-73162-903-6 (e-Book)
ISBN 978-1-73163-339-2 (ePub)
Library of Congress Control Number: 2019944961

Rourke Educational Media
Printed in the United States of America,
North Mankato, Minnesota